Acorn Adventures

Shane Svorec

Acorn Adventures © 2024 by Shane Svorec. All rights reserved.
Written by: Shane Svorec
Illustrated by: Vivien Sárkány
Edited by: Jill Armijo
Author Photo: Susan Teplinsky

Published by SGS Consultants
Hillsdale, NJ

www.shanesvorec.com

All rights reserved. This book contains material protected under International and Federal Copyright Laws and Treaties. Any unauthorized reprint or use of this material is prohibited. No part of this book may be reproduced or transmitted in any form or by any means, electronic or mechanical, including photocopying, recording, or by any information storage and retrieval system, without express written permission from the author.

Library of Congress Control Number: 2024908236
ISBN: 979-8-9903354-2-4 (paperback)
ISBN: 979-8-9903354-1-7 (hardback)

Available in paperback and hardback

Dedication

To all the children we've fostered,
loved, and cared for over the years,
including our own, may you always have
a safe place to grow and a place to call home.
Like an acorn, the places you go may not
be where you stay, but a little love
will help you find your way.

Special Thanks

Many people contributed to this book by being a
special part of my life or a helping hand along the way.
Growing up in many new and unfamiliar places, like an acorn,
the adventures and all those who were part of them became
some of the most unexpected gifts as I learned to embrace
change and appreciate those I met. Life is full of surprises,
but our determination to grow is up to us.

One sunny day, a little acorn fell from a tree.
He plopped on the grass and bounced a couple of feet.

He sat, and he wondered, "Where could I be?
"Beneath me is soft, and all around me is green."

There sat the acorn, round and brown,
With a cap on his head
and his stem upside down.

The sun felt warm, and its light was bright.
The little acorn rested after falling from such a height.

Just then, the wind started to blow,
and the sky began to sprinkle.
When raindrops trickled upon his head,
The acorn giggled, "Ooh, this kind of tickles."

But the rain fell harder, and the sky grew dark. The little acorn wondered if his journey was over or about to start.

Then, suddenly, the birds started to sing,
and the sun came out again.
The worms were busy inching along,
And the butterflies fluttered above his head.

As he sat, he wondered,
"What am I to do? Is this where I belong?
"Are there others here like me, too?"

Just then, a squirrel came along
and plucked him right up.
The squirrel ran so quickly
That the acorn felt only the wind as it rushed.

Tucked inside her cheek, the squirrel scurried up a tree. When they reached the top, the little acorn announced, "This is my home! This is my tree!"

But the squirrel dropped the acorn, and again,
He fell far from the tree.
"Thump!" was his sound after letting out a long
"Wheeeee!"

Back in the blanket of green, the little acorn sat
Until another squirrel snatched him up
and began to run fast.

This time, the squirrel scurried
further away onto a new path.
Quickly, the squirrel traveled,
Holding tightly to the little acorn she had stashed.

The ground was different here and not as soft.
It was rough and dark.
He heard strange noises in this new spot.

Some went "vroom,"
and some brought a fast breeze.
Something screeched,
and he heard many loud beeps.

The squirrel zigged and zagged
and ran forward and back.
She ran in such a hurry
She dropped the little acorn along the path.

The little acorn grew scared
as he hit the ground and rolled.
There was no comfy green grass to rest in,
And nowhere to hide on the busy road.

Just then, a car whizzed by
close to the little acorn.
"Hey! You almost hit me!" he cried,
As he began rolling more.

He rolled to the side and through cracks and puddles.
He rolled fast, and he rolled slow, and when he stopped,
The little acorn knew he was in trouble.

Now, above him were busy feet coming and going. The little acorn worried each time a shadow was showing.

But happy giggles and smiling faces
Soon greeted the acorn that rolled into their path.
Their playful little feet brought him to a quiet place,
And the acorn breathed a sigh of relief at last.

Happy to be in this new place, the little acorn said,
"Is this where I belong?
"I hope I can rest here for a little while
So I can grow big and strong."

The giggling got quieter, and soon it was no longer heard.
But a new visitor prowled and loudly purred.

With a swat here and a swat there,
A *fluffy* cat batted at the acorn,
And she boldly stared.

With long, thin whiskers and many sharp teeth,
The acorn worried she might not be playing,
But instead, the cat wanted to eat!

But she started to roll in the green grass and bathe in the sun. The acorn wasn't dinner; he was just some round fun.

As the acorn sat longer and longer,
He settled into a comfy spot.
Safe beneath the green blanket,
Warm with the sun shining atop.

The weather started to change;
The little acorn felt heavy and secure.
The cat still rolled about, and giggling was heard.

Days turned into night, and soon,
yellow leaves began to fall.
Winter came, and snow fell,
but the little acorn was cozy
And growing strong.

By the time spring arrived,
The little acorn could tell he had grown bigger.
He was much tougher and heavier now,
And his new roots grew deeper!

Becoming a sapling brought new worries and fears.
Lawnmowers came scarily close,
And busy feet carelessly stomped near.

The wind, at times, would howl,
And he held tight to the ground.
His roots outstretched firmly beneath the earth
As his little leaves shook and swayed all around.

As the days went on, his branches began to multiply
His leaves would come and go with the seasons,
His limbs became home to those who fly.

Nests were built, and soon, chirping could be heard.
Little birds took flight from his branches,
And later returned and proudly perched.

Squirrels busily climbed up and down his growing trunk
As they collected and stashed their food.
It wasn't long ago when he was a little acorn
Stuffed inside the cheek of a hungry squirrel, too.

As he started to shoot further up, his playful, giggling
friends grew, too.
When they were no longer little,
The acorn remembered seeing their little shoes.

"They brought me to this spot, and
"I settled into the place where I belonged.
"I'm no longer a little acorn,
"But a big oak tree that has grown acorns of my own."

"When the time comes,
and acorns drop from the tree I've grown to be,
"I hope their journeys lead them to places where they,
too, can grow free."

So, when you spot an acorn,
Remember, each one has had an adventure to be told.
Where they drop, they may not stay,
But a little love helps them grow.

From acorns to saplings to gigantic oak trees,
Sometimes, new faces and unfamiliar spaces
Help us grow and become the best we can be.

The adventure is just the beginning.
The story, like a tree, continues to grow.
How a little acorn can change the world,
Only gigantic oak trees (and now you) know!

About the Author

Shane Svorec is a lifelong writer who loves tenderly stringing words together to capture real emotions and create genuine connections. Her expressive writing touches hearts of all ages, provoking wonder, igniting empathy, and fostering understanding. Shane aims to rekindle the joys of appreciating the simple things in life and believes everyone can make a difference in this world and the life of another. She frequently delivers inspirational talks, loves adventures, and enjoys working with children and animal advocacy groups.

Shane lives in Northern New Jersey but spends much of her time in the Adirondacks with her husband, three children, rescue dog, and chicken.

Svorec's works include the award-winning *Broken Little Believer* and *The Busy Bridge That Got Its Break*.

Milton Keynes UK
Ingram Content Group UK Ltd.
UKHW051207310824
447531UK00017B/17